CATCHING CHRISTMAS DINNER

VICTORIA MATTSEN CRIME SERIES
BOOK 0.5

IFEANYI ESIMAI

ShotReads

Published by ShotReads

eISBN - 978-1-63589-770-8

Stores QR code

Cover by coveredbymelinda.com

Get a FREE copy of The Rookie!

Join my reader group for updates, giveaways, teasers, and a FREE copy of the prequel - The Rookie. Click here or scan the QR code

PROLOGUE

Amelia smiled and walked faster—stolen kisses and stolen moments were always the sweetest. She'd swapped her scrubs for black leggings and a puffy blue jacket over a white sweater. A cream woolly beanie held her blonde hair in place. Amelia had every reason to smile—at twenty-six, she was way ahead of her five-year plan. She was in a career she enjoyed, had more money than she ever dreamed of, and had found love.

Yes, she found love where she wasn't expecting it. Little Amelia Pollock, the most unlikely to succeed girl in her high school graduating class, had a bank account with seven figures. Who'd believe that?

She chuckled. "Eat your heart out, Mrs. Stiff." She had been her high school's guidance counselor. Instead of encouraging Amelia to work harder and improve, she guided her to do less and accept that she'd be stocking shelves at the local grocery store for the rest of her life.

Amelia admired the Christmas lights on some trees and shrubs as she passed by. Some without decorations, their branches devoid of leaves, looked more like trees with their roots in the air—turned upside down. That had been her five years ago. She'd come a long way in a short time.

She raised her head and took a deep breath. The air was crisp, with a faint smell of burning wood and cinnamon. The Christmas song, "Jingle Bells," being performed by the a cappella group she had seen near the entrance before she'd slipped into the park, drifted in and out with the wind. They switched to "Don't Save It All for Christmas Day" by Celine Dion. In that moment, Amelia felt they were singing for her.

Amelia headed for Lovers Patch, nicknamed after the many flower bushes that provided cover for audacious lovers making out on the park bench in the spring and summer. The hedges, with their coating of glistening snow, looked like tiny white mountains.

A smile tugged the corner of her lips—her skin tingled. *Celine can do whatever she wants, she wasn't going to save it all for Christmas Day.*

Amelia's smile faded as an incredible urge to relieve her bladder resurfaced. She'd been putting off peeing, but she had to go now. Maybe it was excitement at the thought of who she was going to meet. Or it could be the result of all those extra cups of coffee she'd had at work to keep her awake. She clenched her muscles and looked around.

Her boots were crunching on the snow as she headed t her destination. Amelia sidestepped a puddle and stood beside the hedges. She looked around, adjusted her handbag that was strung over her shoulder, then ducked.

Amelia relieved herself. Her bare ass—displaying the interlaced heart-shaped tattoo she'd had inked at Hopatcong —shivered in a wind that felt like ice picks against her exposed skin. She chuckled. *I'm painting the snow yellow.* The relief was immediate. She let out a sigh.

Hitching up her leggings, Amelia straightened her clothing and continued to her meeting spot, feet away.

The park bench, hidden from the footpath by flowers and bushes in spring and summer, was visible. Someone had brushed snow off it.

Something snapped, like someone had stepped on a dry twig.

Amelia whirled.

There was nobody—only shadows cast by the park's lamps.

She giggled. "Are you here already? I hope you didn't see me being naughty?"

Her iPhone vibrated in her handbag, then began to ring. She fished it out and looked at the screen. "Christ." She swiped to answer. "Hello, Mother."

"I've been trying to reach you."

Typical, she never asks how I'm doing. "Mother, I got out of work a few minutes ago." Amelia had to make this quick. "Mom, can I call you—"

From her periphery, something hurtled toward her. Amelia spun, gasped, lost her footing, and crashed into the snow.

A barn owl with wings outstretched, claws extended like the landing gear of an Airbus coming in to touch down at Newark's Liberty International Airport, dropped at the base of a snow-covered flower hedge.

Within a second, it rose into the air, the silhouette of a mouse in its claws. The loud screech it let out provided a chorus to the distant sound of "Jingle Bells" from the Christmas carol singers.

Amelia watched the bird disappear into the night. "Wow."

"Hello? Hello?"

Amelia glanced at where the sound was coming from. Her

phone was at the edge of a puddle. She quickly retrieved it, got to her feet, and brushed herself off. "Sorry, Mother, I dropped my phone."

"What was that sound?"

Amelia laughed. "I'm at the park. It was an owl getting its Christmas dinner." She laughed some more, tickled by her joke. "Don't worry. I'll be home for Christmas, and I have a surprise for you. I'll call you later." She hung up before her mother's inevitable questions could follow.

The sound of rushing footsteps behind her caused Amelia to turn. Something hard smashed into her head. Pain exploded inside her skull. The number of twinkling lights on the trees doubled and brightened. Then they faded as she descended into darkness. Her last thought was that the new year fireworks celebration had come early.

1

———

VIKKI MATTSEN SHOWERED and dressed fast. Black pants with a gray sweater top. She'd draped her suit over the back of the dining chair. Her Glock was in her belt holster, and she'd clipped her badge on the other side. She'd retrieved them from her safe, where she kept them when she brought home company.

She glanced at her bedroom door, pursed her lips, then looked away. Vikki hoped her companion for the night would wake up and leave. *Didn't he say he has an early plane to catch?* She didn't want to wake him up and make it more awkward than it already was.

It was all about those fleeting few seconds, where you're still entangled with the other after you metaphorically jumped off the cliff quite willingly. Your heartbeat slows, your chest is still heaving, and you've just about caught your breath. Then clarity returns, dragging its twin—regret—with it.

Vikki always lied to herself about why she picked up men —it was for that release. But deep down, she knew she was punishing herself for what happened in her rookie year. It had been six years, but Vikki still blamed herself. She had shied away from long-term relationships since.

She went to the kitchen to brew coffee. *Maybe the smell will wake him up, so I can usher him out of the apartment.* Vikki rinsed out the reservoir to kill time, then filled it with water. Once it was hot, she added the K-Cup coffee pod. The machine hissed and rumbled, and dark brown liquid dribbled from its spout. Vikki raised her head and inhaled the aroma of French Vanilla, the cobwebs of sleep falling from her eyes.

Vikki had assumed taking the job in a small town would give her time to investigate the murder of her friend, Alexis Devoe, and her father, Mike Devoe. But things got busy in small towns, too. She pushed the thought to the back-burner.

She removed her cup and sipped, rolling the black, burnt, bitter-sweet-tasting liquid in her mouth.

"My god!" said a voice from her bedroom door.

Vikki turned. It was Alex, the traveling salesman she had chatted with at the bar last night and then brought back home.

"You're a cop! Cool! Do you have handcuffs?" His grin turned into a smile.

Vikki added embarrassment to the regret she felt. She maintained her poker face. "Don't you have a plane to catch in an hour from Morristown Airport?"

"Shit," Alex said. He rushed back to the room.

Vikki called a cab for him.

Two minutes later, he was out of the bedroom, fully dressed in jeans, a white button-down shirt, and a blazer. "I have to get my luggage from the hotel."

"Your cab is waiting for you downstairs. You had better get going. You might still make the flight."

Alex opened the door and turned. "Can I see you again when I'm in this neck of the woods?"

Vikki rested a hand on her hip, close to her gun. "It's not a good idea."

Alex fixed his eyes on her hips. "All right then." He opened the door and left.

She let out a sigh of relief. *This is the last time I bring a one-night stand home.*

Vikki's phone rang. "Thank goodness," she muttered under her breath, "Gomez to the rescue." She looked at her phone—it was Detective Pence. She sighed, remembering her regular partner, Mike Gomez, was on vacation. He'd traveled with his wife to spend Christmas with their daughter in California.

Gomez had said, "It's about time I spend Christmas without snow." It was also a practice run for what he'd be doing after he retired in a year.

"Mattsen."

"Morning, Mattsen, Captain Levin asked me to call you," Pence said. He spoke rapidly, not giving her a chance to return his greeting. "We have a situation at Lincoln Park."

"What type of situation?"

"A jogger discovered the dead body of a female this morning. We already have uniforms at the scene. The captain wants you to lead."

Vikki and Pence graduated the same year from the academy, but Vikki's upward trajectory had risen faster. With her regular partner Gomez out, she hoped it wouldn't generate friction between them, even though Pence was leaving for another job in the New Year.

She walked to the window and looked down. A yellow cab was driving away from the apartment complex. Vikki let out a sigh of relief.

"Mattsen?" Detective Pence prompted.

"Yes, I'll be there."

2

____

Vikki walked beside Pence toward the taped-off crime scene. It was 8 a.m. They both wore CSOs—crime scene overalls—over their clothing, and booties over their shoes. She glanced around, taking in the fresh layer of snow that had fallen the night before, and shook her head. It would cover any footprints or evidence left during the attack.

Pence pointed at a distraught woman wearing black and red athletic jogging gear, talking to a uniform. "An early morning jogger discovered the VIC. She said she runs this route five days a week."

The woman wrapped her hands around her body to stop the shaking. Vikki hoped she wasn't going into hypothermia. She knew runners had many hi-tech clothes to keep them warm, but with shock added into the mix, it wouldn't be good for her.

She looked around and noted the gas station across from the park. She hoped they had CCTV pointed at their surroundings and not only at their pumps.

Crime scene investigators were there in their CSOs—CSI written on their vests gave them away. One was taking pictures, and the other was combing the periphery, sweeping for evidence. He'd look for fingerprints, fibers—anything interesting on the victim's clothing.

A uniform handed Vikki a logbook, and she signed it.

Pence lifted the police tape, and Vikki slipped under. He then lowered his six-foot-two frame under the yellow police tape. His crewcut and clean-shaven face made him look five years younger than his actual age of thirty-four.

Vikki looked at the blonde lying prone. Her palms were face down by her side, as if she were sleeping. "Any ID?"

"Yes, we found her handbag," Pence said.

Vikki's eyes shifted to the surroundings. The fresh footprints in the snow close to a puddle of slushy water probably belonged to the jogger.

She put on gloves, bent down, and picked up a long brown feather from underneath a flower hedge. It had a unique pattern on it. She placed it in an evidence bag, wondering if she was overreacting *It's only a feather.* "Was robbery the motive?"

Pence inhaled and then exhaled abruptly. "I don't think so. Credit cards and about five hundred dollars in cash were in her wallet."

Vikki nodded. "That's a lot of money to be carrying around. Easy pickings, yet not picked."

"Her driver's license identifies her as Amelia Pollock," Pence said. "She lives at 274 Canal Street here in St. Ives. We also found a hospital ID. She worked as an ER nurse at the medical center in Milton."

Vikki nodded. "What else is there, if robbery wasn't the motive?"

Pence shrugged. "Jealousy, being in the wrong place at the wrong time. A lovers squabble gone wrong. You—"

"Hello, Detective Mattsen," said a familiar voice in faint,

Indian-accented English, cutting Pence off.

Vikki turned, expecting to see the smiling face of the gray-haired medical examiner. His protective gear covered him from head to toe.

"Hello, Dr. Patel. Good to see you."

Dr. Patel looked around. "I see Detective Gomez is not here. Still on vacation?"

Vikki nodded.

One investigator walked over and said they were done.

Dr. Patel turned to Vikki. "Give me a few minutes for the time of death. I'll need to get the ambient and liver temperatures and do some math."

Vikki didn't want to watch Dr. Patel get the victim's core temperature. She walked over to an investigator. Pence followed.

"We think it was a surprise attack. Blunt force trauma to the head," the investigator said. "Based on how she fell, she probably turned when she heard her assailant. The ME will tell us more after the autopsy."

"I'll have some uniforms comb the vicinity to see if there are any suspicious objects around," Pence said.

Vikki thanked the investigator and glanced over at Dr. Patel. He waved them toward him.

Raising her eyebrows, Vikki asked, "You have a time of death?"

"I'll have to take her to the lab for more investigation," Dr. Patel said. "Rigor mortis has already set in. With the temperature calibration, I'd say sometime between 10 p.m. and 1 a.m. I'll call you once I'm done with the autopsy."

Vikki and Pence would split the workload. Christmas was coming, and the captain and mayor always wanted loose ends tied up quickly. Pence would identify the next of kin from the DMV database and notify them.

3

———————

Vikki parked her cruiser in front of 274 Canal Road. It was an apartment complex, and the victim lived on the second floor. The time on the cruiser's dashboard was 10 a.m.

She flashed her badge and introduced herself as Detective Mattsen to the apartment's receptionist.

"The last time I saw her was yesterday morning," said the receptionist, a twenty-something young man. He spoke English with an Eastern European accent.

Vikki had attended college in France and encountered people there that sounded similar. "Moscow? Kyiv?"

"Kyiv. Is there a problem?"

"Nope," Vikki said. "We're investigating a homicide, Amelia Pollock."

His hand flew to his mouth. "Homicide? What happened?"

"The investigation is ongoing," Vikki said. "Does she get visitors? Boyfriends? Girlfriends? Is there anyone you think might want to hurt Amelia?"

"No. She gets along with everyone," he answered, still referring to her in the present tense.

"Can I see her apartment?"

He hesitated. "Not without a warrant. What if she comes back and sues us for invading her privacy?"

Vikki shook her head. "She's not coming back. Let's say it's a welfare check."

The receptionist said nothing. He went to the back office and returned with a key. He placed it on the counter. "Sometimes she doesn't lock her door. Maybe today is your lucky day, and it's open."

Amelia Pollock's one-bedroom apartment was neat and simply furnished. The living room contained a baby blue couch and a coffee table. A book about owls was next to a laptop computer on a writing desk. An expensive-looking DSLR camera on a tripod pointed out the window. *Maybe she was an avid bird watcher.*

Vikki looked through Amelia's closet and opened several drawers. She had few clothes, but a lot of sexy lingerie. Vikki found nothing out of the ordinary.

4

───────────

TEN MINUTES LATER, Vikki was on her way to see Jenna Richard. Amelia had listed her as a person to contact in terms of emergencies in her apartment application.

Jenna and her boyfriend, Peter Mellon, sat on the three-seater couch opposite Vikki in their apartment living room. There was a real Christmas tree in the corner. Each of their faces showed both shock and sadness.

"When was the last time you saw Amelia?" Vikki asked. She glanced from Jenna to Peter.

"She was here last week," Jenna said. "I can't believe it." Jenna shifted her blonde hair with highlights behind her ears. Tears streamed down her round cheeks. "She's my oldest friend. I encouraged her to move to St. Ives from Highland Falls. She lived with us until she got on her feet. How am I going to tell her mother?"

Peter shook his head and drew Jenna closer. Vikki thought that his square jaw, green eyes, and athletic build put him in another league to Jenna's double chin, full figure, and buck teeth. He mourned quietly.

"She was here one second and gone the next," Jenna said.

Vikki knew what Jenna meant. Her own experiences came to mind. With murder or car accident deaths, friends and relatives never get a heads up. *It is hard.* She set the thought aside. "Does she have any other family or friends here apart from you guys?"

Jenna sniffed. "Her mother lives in Highland, New York. I'll call her. Maybe friends from work."

Vikki hoped Pence had called Highland, New York Police Station and asked them to send over an officer to notify Mrs. Pollock in person.

"Is there anyone you think could have wanted to hurt her?"

The answer was the same—Amelia got along with everyone. Amelia was a real Miss Congeniality.

Vikki said, "Jenna, Peter, I'm going to ask a few questions. These are routine questions I must ask."

Jenna wiped her eyes with the back of her hand. "I understand."

Peter nodded.

"Where were you between 10 p.m. and 1 a.m.?"

Jenna turned to her boyfriend, then glanced back at Vikki. "We were home."

"Can anyone verify that?"

Jenna gave a helpless shrug.

Vikki left her business card. She'd come back in a heartbeat if the investigation led leads back to them. "Call me if you remember or hear anything."

The next stop was the hospital where Amelia worked. On her way, Vikki called Pence to find out how his investigation was going. They'd divided the tasks. He was reviewing the collected video footage.

"I'm still reviewing the CCTV cameras from the gas station. Nothing yet," said Pence.

"I got nothing significant in her apartment or from the friends she listed as next of kin. I'm heading to the medical center."

5

———

THE MILTON MEDICAL CENTER reception area looked like a five-star hotel lobby. A chandelier hung from the ceiling, overlooking different sitting arrangements with couches and coffee tables.

Patients, visitors, and well-wishers came and went. Two kids stood in front of a tall Christmas tree in a corner close to a fireplace. It sparkled and twinkled as the lights turned on and off. Store-bought and handmade decorations hung from it. Its base, covered with wrapped gifts and fake snow, looked as if it could be fresh from Santa's living room.

Vikki stood behind a two-person line waiting for the receptionist. She nodded along to an instrumental rendition of "All I Want for Christmas Is You" playing faintly in the background. Now and then, a voice came over the loudspeakers.

She introduced herself and showed her badge when it was her turn. The sweet old lady told her Mr. Benson, chief of security for the hospital, was the best person to talk to. She called ahead and gave her directions to the security department in the basement.

Vikki introduced herself to Mr. Benson in his claustrophobic office. It had a panel of monitors on one wall, a shelf filled with folders on another, a central desk with a computer, and cardboard boxes piled on the floor. He knew the last chief of police of SIPD and was happy to help. She informed him why she was there.

"I'm so sorry to hear that," Mr. Benson said. "I don't think her unit knows. But let's get to your investigation first. You want to know what time she left the hospital yesterday?"

Vikki nodded. "Hopefully, we can find out the last person who saw her alive."

Mr. Benson made a few calls, then said, "She left her station at the ER after 8 p.m." He typed on the computer, then pointed at the first monitor on the panel. "Miss Pollock was at the ATM in the lobby at exactly five minutes after eight."

Amelia Pollock appeared on the screen—happy, full of life. Vikki's heart felt heavy. She was watching the last hours of Pollock's life. Amelia, dressed in blue scrubs, walked into the lobby. She went to the ATM, spent a few minutes there, then walked back to the elevator.

Mr. Benson fast-forwarded it. "She finally left for good at about twenty minutes after eight." Another video of Amelia appeared. This time she dressed in black leggings and a puffy blue jacket over a white sweater.

Vikki's heartbeat picked up a notch. *Amelia died in that outfit.* She crossed the lobby, headed toward the hospital exit, and then out of camera range.

Mr. Benson typed some commands, and Amelia's image reappeared on the screen. A camera outside focused on the door.

"There she is again," Mr. Benson said.

Another camera picked her up, talking to a woman outside the hospital entrance.

They talked, then walked into the parking lot out of camera range. *Was that her killer?*

Vikki's pulse raced. "Can you zoom in on the other person? It seems like she was waiting for her."

"I'll do better." Mr. Benson moved the mouse around, placed a square over the face, and captured it. A few clicks later, a printer next to him came to life and printed the image.

Vikki stared at the image. "Does she work here?"

"I can't say for sure. But if anyone should know, that would be Molly, the receptionist. She's been here long enough." He rose from his chair. "Come."

"Oh, that's Melissa Dickens," Molly said. "She's a nurse aide. Covers the emergency room."

After a few calls from the hospital lobby, Mr. Benson said, "Melissa is not here today, either. She called in sick this morning."

Very convenient. Warning bells went off in Vikki's head. She got Melissa Dickens's information from Mr. Benson and sent it in a text to Pence. Then she called him.

Pence answered on the first ring. "I got your text—a person of interest?"

"Yes, she met our VIC in the parking lot around 8.30 p.m. Dr. Patel placed the time of death between 10 p.m. and 1 a.m. We want to talk to her. She's not at work. Called in sick."

"You are closer to her location. Send some uniforms to the address to bring her in. I'll meet you at the station."

6

———————

Vikki watched Melissa Dickens through the one-way window in interview room one. According to her DMV database, she was twenty-three and six feet tall. She looked like a model dressed in jeans, a blue sweatshirt, and a puffy orange jacket. Her blonde hair was in a ponytail, and she had duffel-sized bags under her bloodshot eyes. She looked pissed.

Her landlady told the uniforms that went to her address that she was traveling. They hauled her out of line at the bus station while waiting for a bus to Newark's Liberty International Airport. She had 3,000 dollars with her. *Was that the money Amelia got from the ATM?* They'd soon find out.

Vikki walked into the interview room with Pence. It was a small room, about sixteen by four feet, with cream-colored walls. It had a table and three chairs. Vikki took the seat opposite Melissa and said, "I'm Detective Victoria Mattsen, and that's my colleague, Detective Pence." She nodded in Pence's direction.

Pence took the seat on Melissa's left.

Melissa had her elbows on the table and stared at Vikki. *If only looks could kill.*

Vikki continued, "How do you—"

"Why am I here?" Melissa asked. Her voice was deep and hoarse.

"You were on camera talking to Amelia Pollock outside Milton Medical Center. Then you were about to skip town." Vikki looked through her notes. "One-way ticket to Utah. Three thousand dollars in cash in your possession."

Melissa shrugged. "So? Is speaking to someone a crime? This is a free country—I can go anywhere I want."

Vikki narrowed her eyes and leaned forward. "Was this how it happened? You saw the money she had with her and marked your time?"

Melissa frowned. "What?"

"You followed her to Lincoln Park, hit her on the head with a blunt instrument, and took the money. You didn't mean to, but unfortunately, you hit her too hard, and she died."

Melissa sprang to her feet. "Amelia's dead?"

Vikki and Pence also stood up, alert.

"Calm down," Pence said. He extended his hand toward her and gave a subtle nod. "Yes, Amelia is dead."

Melissa crumpled. Tears sprang from her eyes. "What happened?"

"We were thinking you'd tell us," Vikki said.

"You think I have something to do with it?" Melissa asked in a voice choked with tears. "Amelia's my friend. She's the only person who believed in my writing. We discussed Christmas plans, and I told her about a writing seminar I'd love to attend. I told her it was expensive and wished Santa would give me that. She said to meet her at the hospital by eight." Melissa wiped her eyes. "She gave me the money and said to go get famous. I didn't kill Amelia. I left her at the car park after Marcus came over."

Vikki threw open her palms. "Who's Marcus?"

"Dr. Marcus Neil. He's an ER doctor."

Vikki wrote the name on her pad. "Where were you between 10 p.m. and 1 a.m.?"

"I was at a party."

7

———————

When Pence approached, Vikki was at her desk about to check Amelia Pollock's financials.

"Melissa's alibi checked out. She was at a house party—slept there until this morning. The occupants of the house were still sleeping when I got there. One showed me a video they shot on their cellphone with Melissa singing karaoke last night."

"What about if she left, committed the crime, then rejoined the party? Nobody being any the wiser," Vikki said.

Pence shook his head. "It's possible, but I don't see her doing it. Anyway, we told her to put her travel on hold. If things change, we'll get her."

"What else do you have?"

"I visited Milton to talk to Dr. Neil at the hospital."

Vikki raised an eyebrow. "Did you?"

Pence folded his arms over his chest and nodded. "Shocked is an understatement of the look on his face when I confronted him. He said she was one of the best ER nurses he'd ever worked with. Your friend, the security chief, confirmed Dr. Neil was in the hospital between 9 p.m. and 1 a.m. the next morning."

Vikki sighed. "I feel we're missing something. We recovered no cellphone from the scene, right?"

"Right."

The phone on Vikki's desk rang. She looked at Pence, raised a finger, and said, "One moment." She picked up the receiver. "Mattsen."

"Hello, Detective. Dr. Patel here."

Vikki knew he must have found something. Her pulse picked up a notch. "Hi, Dr. Patel."

"I have some results for you," Dr. Patel said in his barely there Indian accent.

"I'll come to the morgue right away."

"No, not now. I'm about to get into a meeting, but you can drop by later. As I said earlier, the time of death was between 10 p.m. and 1 a.m. The cause of death remains as blunt force trauma. She died an hour or two after having sex."

Vikki's insides tightened. She visualized the scene she had seen that morning in her mind's eye. The girl was lying prone. There'd been no sign of a struggle. "Was she raped?"

"I don't think so," Dr. Patel said, his voice cautious. "No bruising, no signs of forced entry, or defensive injuries."

"But coercion or blackmail will not show signs of forced entry," Vikki said.

"True, so I leave it to you as the detective. I recovered DNA. The lab is analyzing it right now. I have to go. Talk later."

Vikki hung up. She turned to Pence and told him what Patel had said.

Pence nodded. "Consensual?"

"Your guess is as good as mine."

Pence inhaled and let out a sigh. "All right, I'll continue

digging through the camera feeds. Something must be there."
He returned to his desk.

Vikki watched Pence go. There was underlying tension, but … She believed in not getting her butter from the same place she got her cheese. Good thing he was leaving for another job.

She shook her mouse to wake her computer. She opened Amelia Pollock's financial statement. Earlier, she'd mentioned to Captain Levin the need to act fast and look at Amelia Pollock's financials. "Not everyone can make a gift of three thousand dollars to a casual friend on a whim."

"Write it up," Levin had said. "I'll have a judge that owes me a favor sign it before he leaves for vacation."

Vikki used a search warrant from an old case as a template and sent it to Levin. Within an hour, she had a warrant, and the bank released the information.

She looked through the statement, starting from January the previous year. Amelia was doing well.

Vikki's stomach rumbled, reminding her she'd skipped breakfast. She went to the break room and got a granola bar from the vending machine. She got a cup of coffee and admired the table Christmas tree someone had placed next to the coffeemaker.

Back to the finances, Vikki noticed a massive spike in Amelia's recorded earnings. Five times her monthly income as a nurse, and it kept growing. The payment came from MeFans Inc.

8

VIKKI HAD HEARD OF ONLYFANS. Was it something similar? She googled MeFans.

MeFans is an online subscription service based in Delaware, where content creators can earn money from users subscribed to their channel.

Registering on the site, Vikki found Amelia's channel and subscribed. There were photos of the victim smiling at the camera, wearing bikinis and lingerie.

She recognized the room in the photos. It was Amelia's apartment. Now she knew the DSLR camera had other uses apart from for watching birds. Her outfits in the pictures explained the drawer full of sexy underwear in her apartment.

Vikki continued to scroll through Amelia's channel. The subscription was tiered, and there was a tab for special requests. Vikki clicked on it. Amelia charged a minimum of 2,000 dollars for special services, and acceptance was at her discretion.

"Detective! I didn't know you were into things like that."

Vikki jumped. Her hand went for her computer monitor. If it were a laptop, she'd have slammed it shut. Heat rushed to her cheeks. "Erm … no. I was only following the victim's financial records."

Pence leaned in. "Isn't that our VIC? She has a MeFans page?" His eyes lingered on the screen. "What a shame. Maybe one of her clients did her. Sorry, wrong choice of words. I mean, killed her."

Vikki clicked the negative sign at the top right corner of her monitor and minimized that screen to the taskbar. It took three attempts to get it. "Maybe one of her clients did, but why? What's the motive? Kill her, and you won't see her parading … doing what she's doing … ever again."

"Get the screen back," Pence said. "I want to see the last time she posted."

Vikki did.

"Click on that one," Pence said, and pointed at the picture with Amelia dressed in a skirt suit. "Look, she's fully clothed —different from the others. Look at the date."

Vikki clicked on Amelia's last episode, from the day before someone had murdered her.

Amelia looked straight at the camera and, in a girly voice, said she was shutting down her MeFans page. She was starting a new phase in her life.

"Starting a new phase in her life," Pence said in a low voice. "But why? She had raving—paying fans. Why close a good thing?"

Smiling, Vikki answered, "Maybe she found religion." Then her face got serious. "She said she was starting a new phase in her life." She read the comments on the video. "Look at what her fans are saying. Some were not ecstatic about it. Maybe one of them took it a step further."

Vikki felt her sixth sense going into overdrive. *The key to breaking the case might lie here.* "We have to look at her MeFans records to get the names of her customers."

"They won't give that up without a subpoena," Pence said.

Vikki wished she'd discovered this lead earlier; she would have asked Levin to help, but now he'd left.

Pence was thoughtful. "Judge Judy Stewart would sign one if she's still here. She hates any form of exploitation of women. Legal or illegal."

"Is there legal exploitation?" Vikki asked.

"Of course, like MeFans. It's exploitation."

Vikki didn't want to argue about that. *People have different reasons for walking the gray area, and from all indications, Amelia did it of her own free will.* "Should I write it up?"

"Don't worry, I'll take care of it. I've worked with her before."

Vikki thanked him. "I'm famished. I'll go to the deli down the road and grab something. Do you want anything?"

Pence shook his head.

"Text me if something comes up," Vikki said, and left.

She grabbed a chicken salad wrap from the deli and wolfed it down. Then her phone buzzed—a text from Pence.

Judge Stewart came through. Info in your inbox.

Vikki brought out her phone, logged into the St. Ives Police Department site, and clicked on the email icon.

9

SHE LOGGED into her email account and opened the files. Amelia Pollock had 2,000 paying fans.

"Jesus," Vikki muttered. She remembered the video she had watched earlier—Amelia's symmetrical, petite body in a bikini, and her voice like a teenager's. She'd had customers from all over the world, both men and women. *Any one of her fans could have turned stalker—if not happy with her retirement.*

Deciding it'd have been easier for local fans to find Amelia if they'd wanted to, Vikki split them by geography. In the US, down to state, county, then town. A familiar name jumped out at her. Dr. Marcus Neil. Username RockMD.

Vikki returned to SIPD and went to Pence's desk.

Pence pulled his eyes away from his monitor. "Did you get my email?" He didn't look so happy to be interrupted.

"Yes, and I found a person of interest."

Pence cocked his head. "Really?"

Vikki smiled and placed a hand on his shoulder. "Goodness, you're tense. Relax, it's not you."

Pence scowled. "Very funny. Who then?"

"Search for RockMD in the document," Vikki said.

Pence's fingers attacked the keyboard. He hit enter, squinted, and drew back. "Dr. Neil?"

Vikki smiled. "Now, that's someone I'd love to talk to."

Pence's eyes narrowed. His jaw clenched. "I asked him if there was anything else. He looked me in the eye and said no." He exhaled noisily through his nose. "We should invite him to SIPD. Have some uniforms bring him over."

10

Dr. Neil sat in interview room two. Vikki glanced at him through the one-way window. He did not look happy.

"Good evening, Dr. Neil. I'm Detective Mattsen. You've already met Detective Pence."

"Yes, I have! What's this nonsense?" he asked, pointing at Pence. "I thought he had cleared me already."

The good doctor was in scrubs. He'd draped his brown, insulated bomber jacket on the table. He was graying at the temples, and boyishly handsome if he wiped the indignation off his face.

"Yes," said Vikki, "until we dug deeper. You didn't tell us the whole truth, RockMD." She stretched the last word out.

Dr. Neil's mouth dropped open. Then he closed it.

"Our investigations led us to Amelia's MeFans page. You've been a very busy boy. You paid for a lot of extra services—one just before she turned up dead. We have evidence that you were the last person to see her alive. You better come clean. DNA recovered from her is being analyzed right now."

The doctor slumped back in his chair. "D-DNA? Please don't tell my wife. The witch will clean me out."

"Dr. Neil, you have bigger problems than your wife finding out," Vikki said. "You are our number one murder suspect."

"Murder? I didn't kill her. She rocked my world."

"Where were you yesterday between 10 p.m. and 1 a.m.?"

"I was at surgery. I-I came in late because … because I dropped Amelia off."

Vikki and Pence exchanged glances.

Adrenalin coursed through Vikki. She took a deep breath and exhaled. "How did she end up in your car?"

"It's a long story," said Dr. Neil.

Pence chuckled. "Doc, we have all day."

Dr. Neil looked resigned. "About a year ago, I subscribed to MeFans. While browsing, I saw a familiar face and subscribed to the channel. Imagine my surprise, it was a nurse I worked with in the ER. I paid for—extra services. Things were good until about a week ago. She said she was shutting down."

Vikki threw out her hands. "Why?"

"She was getting married."

"Married?" said Vikki and Pence in unison.

Dr. Neil shrugged. "That was exactly my reaction. She also gave notice to the hospital. Then I ran into her in the parking lot last night." Dr. Neil inhaled. He expelled the air with a shudder. "She said it was her last day. I asked for a special service. She said it was over. I pressed. She agreed to one last special request for a fat fee. Our relationship was transactional. She sent me a link. I paid right away." His voice grew quiet. "We had sex in my car—then I dropped her off."

"At what time?" Vikki asked.

"Around 9 p.m. or just before. I barely made it to surgery."

"Where did you take her?" Pence asked. "Did anyone see you drop her off?"

"I don't know! I remember she got a text, then told me to drop her at Lincoln Park. You should focus on finding whoever she met at Lincoln Park."

11

———————

VIKKI STOOD in front of a dry-erase board, trying to make sense of the puzzle. Earlier, she'd written some salient points.

Pence picked up a marker and walked up to the board. "She closes her very lucrative side hustle, won't see her best-paying fan anymore, and quits her job." He draws a line across each one he eliminated.

Vikki tapped a finger against her lips.

Pence exhaled. "What would make a woman do something like that?"

"Threat to her life. Boredom," Vikki said. "Oh, she said she was getting married, so maybe love."

Pence threw out his hands. "But to who?"

Vikki rubbed her hands together. "The text she got. Where was her phone? There was no phone at the scene, right?"

"We went through the place with a fine-tooth comb," said Pence. "Maybe the murderer took it. That would be the most logical thing to do."

"I feel we're so close." Vikki raised her hands, then dropped them by her side. "I can't think anymore." She

29

looked at the wall clock. It was 8 p.m. "Let's start over again tomorrow."

12

———

On her way home, Vikki swung by Jenna Richard's apartment. She needed Amelia's phone number.

"Detective, anything new?" asked a surprised Jenna when she opened the door and saw Vikki.

"No, I just wanted to go over some questions again."

"Sure, come in." Jenna held the door open. Vikki walked in and noticed the fresh addition. "That's a big barn owl. It wasn't here earlier?"

"No. I've always had it. Peter bought a stand for it and left it in the car forever. He mounted it not too long ago. Isn't it beautiful?"

Vikki nodded. "It looks so real."

"It is—taxidermy."

Vikki extended her hands out. "Wow. With its wings spread out, it's impressive." She glanced around. "What about Peter?"

"He took Amelia's death so hard. He took something to help him sleep." Jenna laughed nervously. "I know it hasn't hit me yet." She pursed her lips, took a sharp inhale, and shook her head. "Amelia and I always loved owls since when we were little. They are interesting birds." She smiled. "Did you know that when they sing, it means something? They hoot to mark their territory and screech to chase off intruders."

"Some kind of bird talk?" Vikki said. "Interesting." She knew Jenna was trying to keep the grief away with her talk.

Jenna smiled. "Can I get you something to drink? Coffee, tea, water?"

Vikki shook her head. All the bird talk had made her forget why she was there. She threw out some random questions as she tried to remember. "Was Amelia happy? Any boyfriend?"

"She was happy. She didn't have time for boyfriends. If she wasn't at the ER, she was at home." Jenna sounded tearful—her lips quivered. "I can't believe she's gone."

"I'm sorry for your loss. I should go. Sorry for dropping by unannounced." Vikki got up and headed for the door. She grabbed the doorknob and remembered why she had dropped by. "I almost forgot. What's Amelia's phone number? We haven't recovered her cellphone yet."

Jenna paused. "Let me get my phone. Nobody stores numbers in their heads anymore." Jenna walked back to the couch and picked up her phone. She tapped on the screen and then rattled off the number.

Vikki repeated it to confirm. "Thanks."

13

———

BACK AT HOME, Vikki went straight to her bedroom. Alex's cologne lingered in the air. She removed the bedsheet, pillowcase, and blanket, and went to the laundry room. She threw a detergent pod into the washing machine and dumped the bedding into the machine. From her linen closet, she took out everything fresh and made the bed.

Vikki brought out her phone, logged into her work dashboard, and opened the file containing Amelia's clients' names, going through the list and hoping another name would jump out at her. After thirty minutes, fatigue crept in, and she got up to make some coffee.

Her mind drifted to her rookie year. *We were supposed to get coffee.* Tears clouded her eyes. She touched the engagement ring she wore as a pendant on a necklace around her neck. It should have been on her finger if only she'd done things differently.

Vikki's phone fell out of her hand and tumbled into the coffeemaker container.

"Shoot." She snatched it out of the water and dried it quickly with her shirt. *Now I'll have to bury the phone in rice grains to dry it.* Vikki headed to the pantry to get rice, then stopped. She had an iPhone. *They're now waterproof, even if they fall into a puddle.*

She cocked her head. There had been a puddle next to Amelia's body at Lincoln Park. *Maybe Amelia's phone fell in there.* Her pulse raced. She knew she must go to the park—Amelia's phone held the key to finding whoever had asked her to meet them.

14

———

IN LESS THAN A MINUTE, Vikki was speeding toward Lincoln Park.

She screeched to a stop, grabbed her gloves, and exited the car.

It was late. A few people were taking leisure strolls around the park. She dashed toward the crime scene, putting on her gloves as she went.

The police tape was still there. Vikki dipped her hand into the puddle. The water was icy, and she shivered. She dragged her hand along the bottom and felt something. Her pulse picked up a notch. It was an iPhone.

Vikki tilted the phone to let the water drip off, then put it in an evidence bag. She pushed the power button through the plastic, and the phone lit up. Excited, she headed to her cruiser.

At the station, Vikki raised an eyebrow when she saw Pence. "You're still here?"

Pence looked up from his computer. "It's only 10 p.m.— working on those camera feeds. I thought you went home?"

Vikki raised the evidence bag.

Pence's eyes widened. "That's her phone? Where did you find it?"

"In an icy puddle at the crime scene."

"I bet it's locked," Pence said. "How do we gain access to it?"

"Go to the morgue."

"Hell no," Pence said, shaking his head. "Dr. Patel wouldn't allow that without a warrant."

"I wish I was still in New York," Vikki muttered under her breath.

"I heard that," said Pence. "That's why I'm moving after Christmas. Working with more resources." He raised a finger. "Have you seen those college grads at the IT forensics lab in action?"

Vikki shook her head. Captain Levin was trying to improve the digital footprint of the department by rotating civilians with computer expertise through the department to help with cyber and digital lawbreaking, and hopefully solve crimes through digital forensics.

"Criminals always embrace new technology and figure out how to exploit the masses with it before the police catch on," Captain Levin had said. "Law enforcement agencies like us can only beat them if we run 'what if' scenarios and come up with the solutions before the criminal acts take place."

"Give me the cell," Pence said. "There's this kid in IT forensics. I'm sure he has a phone analyzer."

Vikki hesitated.

Pence laughed. "We're on the same team, remember?"

She gave it to him.

"I'll be right back," Pence said, and headed for the door.

Vikki wanted to follow, but it would be obvious she didn't feel comfortable with him walking away with their smoking gun. She restrained herself. Instead, she stayed on her computer, going through the file from MeFans. She was looking for any names that might jump out at her.

Pence returned with the phone twenty minutes later. A faint smell of formalin hung around him. Vikki wondered why he smelled like the morgue. Then he gave her the phone, and that thought ended there.

"It's open!"

"I've been tapping the screen to stop it from locking," Pence said. "You'll have to do that, or we're back to where we started."

Vikki had a better idea; she opened the map icon, typed in her address, and hit go.

"Make a left on Main Street," said a map navigation voice in posh English accent.

Pence laughed, shaking his head. "She changed hers to a sexy male voice." He glanced at Vikki. "As long as the map direction is on, the lock screen won't come on—genius!"

Vikki knew the phone wouldn't be admissible evidence in any court, but she hoped they'd find a lead or two from the text to figure out what had happened to Amelia. She tapped on the text message icon.

The text inviting Amelia Pollock to the park sat there waiting like a snowman in the backyard. She wrote down the number.

"Let me see that," Pence said. He typed the number into his cell and called it. It gave a busy tone. "I thought as much. It's a burner. The number is like a batch from my last case."

Looking at the phone's call log, Vikki found that the last one was from an area code 845 number, at 9.45 p.m. the previous day. It lasted one minute and ten seconds.

Vikki called the number on her phone.

"Lia!" a woman said.

Vikki explained she was the police. A lump formed in her throat when the woman said she was Amelia's mother.

"I'm sorry for your loss," Vikki said. "We're trying to find out what happened to your daughter. Is it okay if I ask you some questions?"

She said it was fine and filled Vikki in on the missing parts.

"Lia was supposed to come home for Christmas," Amelia's mother said in a tear-choked voice. "The last time we talked, she was at the park. The phone dropped from her hand at one point."

"How?"

Amelia's mother laughed. "She said an owl had swooped down close to her to grab its Christmas dinner, startling her. Then she said she had to go and hung up. She sounded like she was meeting someone. I didn't get to say goodbye." The woman sobbed.

Vikki repeated how sorry she was and hung up. Talking to the woman had ripped her heart apart. She told Pence what the woman had said.

"An owl scared her?" Pence said.

Vikki nodded. "I think Amelia was into owls." She remembered the book in her apartment.

Amelia's phone rang.

Vikki and Pence froze.

Pence reached for it. "Should we answer it?"

Vikki placed a hand on his. "Wait."

The ringing stopped. Vikki reached for it—it rang again, the same number.

Pence wrote the number on an envelope on Vikki's table. "Let me see if those computer guys can find the location." He rushed out of the room.

Vikki's mind bounced from idea to idea. Amelia's phone

would ring, then cut off. Ring and cut off. She did that, too, when searching for her phone in her apartment. She'd call with the home phone and listen to hear her phone ringing. Someone was looking for Amelia's phone.

She grabbed her peacoat from the back of her chair. She knew where the call was coming from.

Pence rushed into the squad room, almost knocking down another detective. "Lincoln Park."

15

———

Vɪᴋᴋɪ, Pence, and two uniforms descended on the deserted, rectangular-shaped Lincoln Park.

A group sang Christmas carols by the entrance. They were not there earlier. Vikki approached from the east and Pence from the west. The uniforms covered the north and south sides, respectively.

Vikki headed for the crime scene where she'd been an hour earlier. She glanced all over as she walked. Then she saw the light from a flashlight. Someone was on their hunches searching the base of the flower hedge.

"Looking for this?" Vikki held up the evidence bag containing Amelia's phone.

Jenna Richard spun around. The flashlight dropped from her hand.

"D-Detective Mattsen. What are you doing here?"

"Why, Jenna? Why did you do it?"

"Do what? I … I don't know what you're talking about."

"You've been calling Amelia's number non-stop with a burner phone, hoping to hear it ring so you can retrieve it. The game is up, Jenna. We read your text. The one you sent from Peter's phone. You invited her here and murdered her."

Jenna turned around and headed in the opposite direction.

Pence emerged from behind a snowbank and blocked her.

The other two deputies blocked each path she tried to take.

Jenna glared at them. "You can't prove anything."

Vikki took a step closer. She'd reckoned the feather she found at the scene came from another owl, but she used it anyway. "Not everyone has a taxidermy barn owl missing a primary feather in their living room. I recovered that feather at the murder scene."

Jenna's mouth dropped open.

"And not everyone has the murder weapon in their living room with a strand of Amelia's hair on it."

Jenna stared at her with eyes as wide as Christmas tree ball ornaments.

Vikki's bluff was working. She needed to drive the nail in and get her to confess. "Why, Jenna? She didn't do you any harm. Why?"

"Because she's a heartless, conniving slut! I took her in. I brought her out of that shitty town, and she repays me by stealing my man. Look at me. I can't compete with her." Jenna let out a shaky breath. "They were going to get married." She spoke in a small voice. Tears streamed down her face.

"That's a relationship problem that shouldn't lead to murder."

Jenna fell to her knees in the snow and sobbed. Tears poured down her face. "He was all in with me until Amelia showed up. All I wanted to do was talk to her. But when that owl scared her, and she fell, I couldn't help myself. I-I had the stand in my hand."

Vikki walked over, removed her cuffs from her belt, and cuffed Jenna without resistance. She read her rights to her. "Jenna Richard, you are under arrest for the murder of Amelia Pollock."

Jenna lowered her head as Vikki read the rest of her rights. She handed her over to the uniforms.

CAPTAIN LEVIN, dressed in a navy-blue suit, white shirt, and red tie, looked at Vikki sitting across his desk in his office. "How did you know the owl stand was the murder weapon?"

"I didn't," Vikki said. "Jenna confessed to that, but she thought I knew. I put two and two together and called her bluff. The stand and the owl weren't there the first time I went to her apartment—and I'd picked up a feather from the crime scene. I erroneously thought the feather came from her taxidermy owl, placing her at the scene. But it seemed there'd been a live owl at the scene based on Amelia's mother's account."

"Let me get this right," Captain Levin said. "Amelia made seven figures from her MeFans page." He cocked his head. "She was also having an affair with her friend's boyfriend, Peter."

Vikki nodded. "They were going to get married, then visit her mother for Christmas."

Captain Levin nodded. "She runs into this doctor in the parking lot, who's her super fan. Then she gets a text supposedly from Peter to meet at the park. But Jenna had sent it with Peter's phone. Ms. Pollock went to Lincoln Park thinking she was meeting Peter. And Ms. Richard came at her with a pipe from her owl stand. Premeditated—she murdered her friend in cold blood."

Vikki nodded. "We'll let the DA come up with a suitable term."

"Where's this Peter now?"

Vikki gave a one-shoulder shrug. "I don't know. We cut him loose after we questioned him. We have nothing on him."

Captain Levin inhaled and exhaled. "Well done, Detective Mattsen. I spoke with Pence earlier. He said he had a plane to catch. What about you? Any plans for Christmas?"

Vikki hesitated. "I'm still thinking about it."

"We're having a few people over for dinner. You can always join us."

Vikki smiled. "I'll think about it, sir, thank you. Merry Christmas."

+++

THE ROOKIE – PREQUEL TO VICTORIA MATTSEN CRIME Series

Outstanding detectives are molded not born—forged through years of hard work, dedication to duty, and hands-on experience. Vikki's first week as a rookie police officer put her on a fast track.

Do you want to know what happened ten to twelve years earlier?

Get a FREE copy of The Rookie!

Join my reader group for updates, giveaways, teasers, and a FREE copy of The Rookie. Click here or on any image below!

THE ROOKIE - PREQUEL
CHAPTER 1

She sat still, knees pressed tight against her chest next to whiskey bottles in the dark kitchen cabinet—whiskey bottles stashed in there to soften her up by a father who loved the taste of whatever his groping hands pulled out.

The smell in the bar—liquor, beer, cigarette smoke, piss—suspended in the air like a kite on a hot spring day reminded her of that cupboard from her childhood. The stink, a blend of liquor spills from indeterminate brands over the years—and when her bladder let go.

Vikki blinked as she tried to adjust to the dim light in the bar. The Sparrow, an Irish pub frequented by the rank and file of the 64th precinct in Brooklyn, New York, was packed.

Too many people. She scanned the faces, not making eye contact. Her stomach muscles were wound so tight her diaphragm refused to move.

"The tough guy act was dropped once we slapped cuffs on him!" said a raspy male voice. "He cried for his mommy!"

This was followed by raucous laughter.

She glanced at the bar where the voice had come from.

The raspy voice belonged to Sean McClane, a Field Training Officer.

FTO for short.

TO for better euphonic sound.

Memories buried deep in her subconscious reared their ugly heads. Time always moved on, but the demons in men remained the same. The same monster inhabiting her father's eyes she'd also seen in McClane's.

Vikki shivered.

"Victoria! Victoria!"

She jerked at the sound of her name. Three raised hands sitting in a booth to her left beckoned to her. A smile parted her lips. Her stomach freed up, and air rushed into her lungs. She headed to their table.

"It took me a minute to realize it was you," said Jenny Lin. "Runway, sit by me." She shifted to her left to make more room.

"You know, you could pass for a model moonlighting as a police officer," said Juan Rodriguez.

"She did that already in Paris!" said Jenny. "Why do you think I call her Runway?"

Vikki was five feet nine inches tall. She'd let her blonde hair down after having it up all day in a ponytail. She had on jeans and a tee shirt. Something different from the police uniform she'd worn all week.

Men and women hit on her. They called her pretty. Maybe on the outside. What would they say when they saw the ugliness inside her? The things she went through as a little girl.

"I should pay more attention to my colleagues," Juan said. "You guys remind me of my pals from high school. Solid friendships."

Juan was twenty-five. He had a Criminal Justice degree

from John Jay College of Criminal Justice. Being a cop was what he always wanted to do.

"Glad you made it," said Ken Wilson. "At least I know you modeled in Paris. After six months at the academy, all our secrets become open secrets."

Vikki smiled at Ken. *Not all of them.* After ten years at a Fortune 500 company, he'd had enough. He had trained subordinates that had elevated to the C suite while he was kept at the same level.

"I decided to take my black ass out of corporate America," Ken had said. "And do something I liked. Alas, all the *isms* were there, too. The fight by people of color for equality is everywhere. But at least now I enjoy what I'm doing, helping people directly while continuing the struggle."

They ordered. Hennessy and Coke for Vikki. Ken, too. Corona for Juan, and a margarita for Jenny.

They ate steak, pasta, and salad for the next thirty minutes and talked about their first week as Rookies. They'd been training and studying their butts off at the New York Police Academy in Queens only a week earlier.

As Juan and Ken argued over basketball, Jenny leaned over to Vikki and said, "What's the deal with you and your Field Training officer?" She jerked her head to the right, chewed, and swallowed. "I thought your TO was supposed to be your trainer, not your friend."

Vikki looked at her TO, Bruce Bruckner, sitting with some other folks she recognized a few tables away. Heat rushed to her cheeks. Sweat trickled down her back.

"I-I knew him before I got here. It's a long story."

"Like knew him, knew him?"

Vikki didn't want to ask what she meant by that or go into detail. "Well, we kind of bumped into each other in traffic a long time ago, and he offered to buy me dinner, and here we are."

"Well, good for you. At least you hit the ground running. But don't they frown on such relationships?"

Vikki recovered fast. "They frown on everything, but you're right." She exhaled noisily. "He's been here longer and knows the best way to navigate these things."

"Hey, guys," Ken said in hushed excitement. "I heard that detective having drinks with your TO." He gave a head nudge in Vikki's direction. "He has the accountant to The Gilbert Organization hidden away somewhere. He's agreed to testify against the CEO of The Gilbert Organization."

The news didn't mean much to Vikki, but Ken's enthusiasm was infectious.

"Once he gives evidence, Mr. Gilbert is going to jail, and his political aspirations will end."

Vikki got up. "I need to use the bathroom."

"Go ahead," Jenny said. "I want to understand what Ken is so excited about."

Vikki's run to the bathroom was uneventful. On her return trip along the narrow hallway lit by a single, dim yellow bulb, a hairy hand blocked her path. It belonged to the man at the bar. His eyes gazed all over Vikki, then settled on her chest.

"Booty Boot, I hear you gave it up to your TO already," McClane said. His words slurred. He smelled of brandy and fresh sports cologne. One of those that were colored blue and had blue in the title. "What about a piece for me."

He cupped Vikki's ass and squeezed. Forced his lips on hers, tongue inside her mouth.

Something in Vikki's head snapped.

...continue reading the Rookie

Get a FREE copy of The Rookie!

Join my reader group for updates, giveaways, teasers,

and a FREE copy of The Rookie. Click here or scan the QR below.

ABOUT THE AUTHOR

Ifeanyi Esimai is a mystery and crime writer and enjoys reading across different genres. When he's not writing or reading, he's exploring documentaries on museums and ancient history.

www.ingramcontent.com/pod-product-compliance
Lightning Source LLC
Chambersburg PA
CBHW070914100726
47907CB00008B/2323